Jeanne Titherington
Where Are You Going, Emma?

Greenwillow Books

New York

« P S A L M S 51:7 »

Colored pencils were used for the full-color art.
The text type is ITC Berkeley Old Style.

Printed in Hong Kong by South China Printing Co.

First Edition   10 9 8 7 6 5 4 3 2 1

Library of Congress Cataloging-in-Publication Data

Titherington, Jeanne.
Where are you going, Emma? / by Jeanne Titherington.
p.   cm.
Summary: Frightened when she wanders too far from her
grandfather as he picks apples in an orchard, Emma is
relieved when he calls her back and they go home together.
ISBN 0-688-07081-7.   ISBN 0-688-07082-5 (lib. bdg.)
[1. Grandfathers—Fiction.]   I. Title.
PZ7.T53Wh 1988   [E]—dc19
87-23298   CIP   AC

TO
THE
ANGELS

Emma and her Grandpa walked to Mr. Barter's orchard to pick apples for Grandma's winter canning.
Grandpa stopped at the first tree, but Emma walked past him.
"Where are you going, Emma?" Grandpa asked.
Emma knew where she was going, but she wasn't going to tell.

Emma was going to climb the orchard's stone wall
to see what was on the other side.
"Just don't go too far!" Grandpa warned.

Emma climbed up the wall and over to
the other side. The first thing she saw
was a tiny brook.
Emma found a pebble.

Next to the brook grew bushes and weeds.
Emma picked a flower.

Beyond the bushes was a small meadow.
Emma pulled up a piece of dry grass
and made a bracelet.

At the far side of the meadow
was a stand of tall oaks.
Emma chose a leaf.
But then she stopped.

Emma looked around.

"Emma! Come back!"

Emma turned to the sound of her Grandpa's voice.

"Here I am, Grandpa! Here I am!"

Leaving the tall oaks behind, Emma ran back through the small meadow, past the bushes and weeds, across the tiny brook, over the stone wall to her Grandpa in the orchard.

When they left the orchard, Emma and Grandpa saw Mr. Barter in the distance, driving his wagonful of apples.

"Where is he going, Grandpa?" Emma asked.

"He must be going home," said Grandpa.

And soon Emma and Grandpa were home, too.